DISNEY

HORSETAIL HOLLOW

AMAZINGLY ANGUS

2

AMAZINGLY ANGUS

By Kiki Thorpe

Illustrated by Laura Catrinella

Los Angeles   New York

First Hardcover Edition, July 2022
First Paperback Edition, July 2022
10 9 8 7 6 5 4 3 2 1
FAC-020093-22147
Printed in the United States of America

This book is set in Goudy Old Style Std/Monotype; Laughing Gull/Atlantic Fonts
Designed by Samantha Krause
Illustrated by Laura Catrinella

Library of Congress Cataloging-in-Publication Data

Names: Thorpe, Kiki, author. • Catrinella, Laura, illustrator.
Title: Amazingly Angus / by Kiki Thorpe ; illustrated by Laura Catrinella.
Description: First edition. • Los Angeles : Disney Hyperion, 2022. • Series: Horsetail hollow ; book 2 • Audience: Ages 5–8. • Audience: Grades 2–3. • Summary: When the Wishing Well sends Merida's horse, Angus, to Horsetail Hollow, sisters Evie and Maddie must find a way to get him back to Merida's fairy tale in order to help her find her happily ever after.
Identifiers: LCCN 2021057040 • ISBN 9781368072250 (hardcover) • ISBN 9781368072281 (paperback) • ISBN 9781368073943 (ebook)
Subjects: CYAC: Characters in literature—Fiction. • Wishing wells—Fiction. • Magic—Fiction. • Horses—Fiction. • Sisters—Fiction. • Princesses—Fiction. • Fairy tales. • LCGFT: Fairy tales.
Classification: LCC PZ7.T3974 Am 2022 • DDC [Fic]—dc23
LC record available at https://lccn.loc.gov/2021057040

Reinforced binding

Visit www.DisneyBooks.com

For Joie and Esther

Maddie Phillips and her little sister, Evie, had a
problem. It wasn't a small one. In fact, the problem
was quite large. Horse-size, to be exact.

Maddie and Evie's problem was the enormous
horse that had suddenly—*magically*—appeared in
their family's barn. All because of a mixed-up wish.

The horse was a handsome black Shire with a
white blaze on his forehead. His mane and tail were

thick and shaggy. Tufts of white hair grew on his fetlocks. They made him look like he was wearing furry boots.

But the most striking thing about the horse was his size. Maddie was nine years old and tall for her age. Her head didn't even come up to the horse's withers.

"Easy, boy." Maddie inched closer to the strange horse. She didn't want to frighten him.

But the horse didn't seem frightened. He gazed down at her with shining black eyes. Then he swished his tail and nickered as if to say, *Well? Now what?*

Evie tipped her head back to look up at him. "Hiya, Angus!" she said with a dimpled smile.

"How do you know his name?" Maddie asked in surprise.

"Because he's *Angus*," Evie said.

Maddie looked at her blankly.

Evie rolled her eyes and sighed. "Princess

Merida's horse! Don't you know *anything* about princesses, Maddie?"

"No," Maddie said. Evie was the princess expert. She knew every fairy tale forward and backward. Maddie had never paid much attention to fairy tales. At least, not until the horses started showing up.

That summer, Maddie, Evie, and their parents had moved to a farm called Horsetail Hollow. On the farm was an old well, and the well was magic! When Maddie and Evie accidentally wished on the same penny, both of their wishes had come halfway true. Maddie had wished for a horse of her own. Evie had wished for a fairy-tale princess for a friend. And the wishing well had brought them . . . a fairy-tale horse.

The horse's name was Maximus, and he had arrived in Horsetail Hollow straight from the pages of "Rapunzel" in Evie's beloved book of fairy tales. At first, Maddie was overjoyed. But then she and Evie realized that Rapunzel's story had changed—there was no more happy ending! So the sisters had to return Maximus to his story so Rapunzel could reach her happily-ever-after.

Now, it seemed, they had another fairy-tale visitor.

"But we only made one wish," Maddie said to Evie. "Why did we get *another* horse?"

"I don't know. But he's the *best* horse." Evie looked at Maddie. "Aren't you gonna pet him?"

Maddie held her hand out to the horse. Angus put his soft nose against it and breathed in. Maddie felt the warm air whoosh out against her fingers. Then he lowered his head trustingly, as if to say, *You're all right.*

Maddie ran a hand down his warm, strong neck. His glossy black fur was soft and smooth. "What are we going to do with you, Angus?" she said softly.

"I thought you wanted a horse," Evie said.

"I did," Maddie said. "I do!"

"Then why don't you look happy?" Evie asked.

Before Maddie could answer, they heard a voice outside. "Maddie? Evie? Are you in there?" It was Mom!

"*That's* why!" Maddie hissed. "What are we

going to tell Mom and Dad? They don't even know Maximus is gone. How are we going to explain a new horse? Quick! Cut her off before she comes in!"

Maddie and Evie scrambled for the door. Maddie turned and pointed a finger at the big horse. "You stay there. Don't make a sound."

Angus snorted.

Maddie and Evie got outside just as Mom reached the door. She was wearing dusty work clothes and her curly hair was tied back.

"There you are. I've been looking all over for you two." Mom folded her arms and raised one eyebrow. "Girls, what is going on?"

"Um . . ." said Maddie.

"Uh . . ." said Evie.

"It's almost noon, and you haven't even started your chores," Mom said.

"Oh, *chores*!" Maddie almost shouted with relief. "Sorry, Mom. We'll get right to it."

"The dishwasher still needs to be unloaded. The porch needs to be swept. And I need you both to help weed the garden." She looked from one sister to the other. "What have you been doing all morning?"

Maddie and Evie exchanged a look. They had spent the morning helping Maximus get back to his fairy tale. They'd galloped through fantastic forests to find the thief who would save Princess Rapunzel from her tower prison. But that seemed like a lot to explain.

"We were reading," Maddie said.

"In the hayloft," Evie added.

Mom's face softened. "It's nice to see you two getting along. But from now on, no reading until chores are done. Got it?"

"Got it," said Maddie.

"Got it," said Evie.

Got it, the horse nickered from inside the barn.

"That reminds me, Maddie," Mom added, glancing at the door. "Don't forget to feed Maximus. He sounds hungry."

"You mean Angus," said Evie, without thinking.

Maddie elbowed her.

"Who's Angus?" Mom asked.

"That's, uh, Maximus's nickname," Maddie said quickly.

Mom looked at her strangely. "Chores," she repeated. Then she walked away.

"Phew!" Maddie said when she was gone. "That was close."

"Hurry! Let's get Angus back to his fairy tale before Mom comes back," Evie whispered.

"Already?" Maddie's heart dropped. "But he just got here."

Evie put her hands on her hips. "Maddie, we have to take Angus back to his story. Princess Merida needs him!"

"I know." Maddie looked at the beautiful horse longingly. "I just thought maybe I'd have a chance to ride him first. And feed him an apple. And maybe braid his hair."

"But the fairy tale—" Evie began.

"The fairy tale won't disappear in an hour, right? Let's just keep him for the afternoon. If we do our chores quickly, we'll have plenty of time to play with him. Then we can take him home before dinner." Maddie petted Angus's mane, already imagining the fun they could have.

"I guess so," Evie said uncertainly.

At that moment, Mom walked back into the barn. "Oh, girls, one more thing—"

When she saw Angus, she stopped in her tracks. "What on earth . . . ?"

Angus shook his forelock out of his eyes and snorted. *Busted*, he seemed to say.

Mom's eyes traveled from the strange horse to

the two girls standing next to him. "Does someone want to tell me what's going on?"

Maddie looked at Evie. Evie looked at Maddie. Their eyes said the same thing.

There was only one thing they *could* tell her. The truth.

CHAPTER
TWO

"So that's why Maximus had to go back to Rapunzel's kingdom. Without him, Rapunzel would have been stuck in her tower forever!" Evie explained.

Maddie, Evie, Mom, and Dad sat on hay bales inside the barn. They had moved Angus into Maximus's old stall, where he was happily eating oats.

"And just when we got Maximus home, Angus turned up. All because of our wish!" Evie went on.

"But don't worry. We were just about to take him back to his fairy tale. So everything is going to be okay."

Mom and Dad stared at Evie. They both looked a little dazed. Evie gave Maddie a thumbs-up as if to say, *This is going great!*

Maddie knew better. From the looks on her parents' faces she could guess what was coming next.

At last, Dad cleared his throat. "Girls, it is truly amazing . . ."

Evie beamed.

". . . that you would sneak a strange horse into the barn, and then make up some wild story about it," Dad finished. "What were the two of you thinking?"

Evie's face fell. "But it's true!" she protested.

"Let's try this again." Mom looked at Maddie. "Where did you find this horse?"

"He just showed up in the barn," Maddie said. "Like Evie said."

Mom frowned. "Maddie, I'm surprised. This isn't like you."

"Me?" Maddie exclaimed. "What about Evie?"

"Evie is six," Mom said. "You are almost ten. I expect you to know better."

Maddie scowled in frustration. Her parents had asked for the truth. But they didn't believe her when she told them. It wasn't fair!

"Girls, this horse belongs to someone," Dad said. "Don't you want to help him get home?"

"That's what I told you!" Evie cried. "We *are* trying to help him get home. He belongs to Princess Merida. And we can prove it!"

Dad raised his eyebrows. "You can?"

"We can?" Maddie echoed.

Evie stood up. Her cheeks were pink, and she looked like she might cry. But her jaw was set. "We'll make a wish at the wishing well. Then you'll see. It *is* magic."

"Evie . . ." Mom began.

Evie folded her arms.

"Oh, all right," Mom said with a sigh. "Let's go see this magic wishing well."

The old well stood a little ways from the barn near a grove of trees. It looked just like a well in a fairy tale. It had a round stone wall and a metal bucket hanging from a little shingled roof.

As Maddie led Angus toward the well, her stomach flip-flopped. What would Mom and Dad say if the wish didn't work? she wondered. And what would they say it if *did*?

At least Angus was no trouble. The horse walked calmly on his lead. At the well he stood patiently, watching everything with bright, curious eyes. Maddie could already tell he was a lot more easygoing than Maximus.

And I never even got to ride him, she thought with a sigh.

When they were all gathered around the well, Evie said, "I almost forgot! We need a penny to make the wish."

Dad dug a coin out of his pocket and handed it to Evie.

Evie squeezed the penny tight in her fist. Maddie put her hand on Evie's.

"What should we wish for?" Maddie asked.

"How about a new pickup truck?" Dad suggested.

Evie ignored him. "We'll wish Angus home," she told Maddie. "Then Mom and Dad will see we were telling the truth."

What would happen? Maddie wondered. Would Angus disappear before their parents' eyes? Or, like last time, would they all be whisked into the fairy tale? Maddie tried to imagine her parents mingling with princesses, witches, kings, and queens. She couldn't.

But Maddie knew one thing for sure. If the wish came true—if Angus did vanish—her parents would freak out. Then they could say good-bye to the wishing well. And Maddie might never get her own horse.

"On the count of three," Evie said.
"One . . . Two . . . Three!"

Maddie closed her eyes and wished. Together, the sisters dropped the penny into the well.

Maddie held her breath. She waited for the wind to blow and the horse-shaped weather vane on the barn to spin. She waited for the world to blur, as it always did when their wishes were granted.

But nothing happened. Not even a breeze stirred the air. Angus shifted and nickered softly.

Evie's eyes were squeezed shut. When she heard Angus, she opened them. "It didn't work." She looked at Maddie. "Why didn't it work?"

"Okay," Mom said. "I think we've had enough fun. Both of you go finish your chores. Dad and I will deal with the horse."

"What are you going to do?" Maddie asked, suddenly worried.

"We need to find his owner," Mom said. "They must be looking for him."

"But he's going to stay here until we find them, right?" Maddie asked.

"We're not running a hotel for lost horses, Maddie," Mom said with a sigh. "He's not our responsibility."

20

"He's lost!" Maddie said. "Where else can he go?"

Mom rubbed her forehead the way she did when she was getting a headache. "Oh, all right. Put him in the barn. Just for now."

Maddie took Angus's lead rope. She quickly led him toward the barn before her mom could change her mind.

Evie ran alongside her. "Why didn't it work?" she asked again. "It always worked before."

"Maybe we ran out of wishes," Maddie said with a shrug.

Evie stopped walking. "Ran out?"

Maddie stopped, too. "In stories, you always get three wishes," she explained. "And that's the number of wishes we made. The first wish brought Maximus. The second wish took us into his fairy tale. And the third wish brought us home. Maybe we used them all up."

Evie looked worried. "Can that happen?"

"Who knows?" Maddie didn't meet Evie's eyes.

21

She started walking again. "Come on, Angus."

Maddie knew the real reason the wish hadn't come true. It hadn't come true because when she closed her eyes, Maddie had made a different wish.

She'd wished for Angus to stay.

"Good morning, Angus!" Maddie called as she came into the barn.

Angus's head poked out of the stall. His black forelock flopped over his face as he nickered in greeting.

Maddie held both of her hands behind her back. "I've got a treat for you. Guess which hand."

Angus nudged her right arm with his nose.

"Good guess." Maddie withdrew her right hand from behind her back. She was holding a carrot.

She started to put the carrot in Angus's trough, then paused. Would he take it from her instead?

She held out the carrot. The horse nibbled it right from her hand.

Maddie's heart melted. She loved the feel of his velvety soft muzzle and the way his chin whiskers tickled her fingers. Maximus had always been too proud to eat from her hand. But Angus was already nosing Maddie's other arm, as if to say, *More, please.*

"Another good guess." Maddie withdrew her left hand from behind her back. She was holding a carrot in that one, too.

As Maddie was feeding the second carrot to Angus, Mom walked into the barn.

"Mom, look! Angus is eating from my hand. I think he really likes me," Maddie said.

"When you're done feeding him, please get started on your chores," Mom said. "I don't want you spending the whole day in the barn again."

Maddie sighed. Spending the day with Angus was exactly what she'd been hoping to do. "What about Evie?" she asked. "Doesn't she have to help?"

"Evie is helping me clean out the old chicken coop," Mom explained. "We're picking up the laying hens tomorrow."

Since they'd moved to Horsetail Hollow, the Phillips family had been working hard to turn the run-down old farm into a homestead. They'd fixed up the farmhouse, planted a garden, and patched the old barn. Little by little, Maddie's parents were making their dream come true.

And now Maddie's dream had come true, too. She scratched under Angus's chin. "Want to pet him, Mom?" she asked. "He's super sweet."

Mom regarded Angus with a frown. "A horse his size must eat a fortune in hay," she said.

"Don't mind her," Maddie told Angus when Mom was gone. "She's usually nice. She's just been kind of grumpy lately."

Both Angus's ears turned toward Maddie. She could tell he was listening.

"I think it's the farm," Maddie explained. "I hear

her and Dad talking at night sometimes. Mom is
worried we took on more than we can handle."

Angus gazed at her with his kind eyes. He sighed,
almost sympathetically.

"You're a good listener," Maddie said. She
wished there was some way she could make Mom
see how great Angus was. "I'm sorry I have to go
right now. I'll get my chores done fast, and then
we can—" Maddie broke off.
"That's it!"

"What is?" Evie asked,
coming into the barn.
She was wearing overalls,
rubber boots, and a plastic
jeweled crown.

"Angus can help with my
chores!" Maddie said. "Once
Mom and Dad see how useful
he is, they'll want to keep
him around."

"Angus?" Evie said doubtfully. "But he's a royal horse."

"So?" said Maddie.

"So he's used to princesses and parades and adventures in the woods. I don't think royal horses do chores," Evie said.

"Angus is a *draft* horse," Maddie replied. "They're made for farmwork." She slipped a halter over Angus's head, then clipped on a lead rope. "Come on, pal. Let's show Mom and Dad what you can do!"

Angus swished his long, shiny tail. He nickered, as if to say, *Lead the way!*

Maddie's first chore was to finish weeding the garden. Weeds and grass had sprouted between the rows of lettuce, carrots, green beans, and peas.

"I'll get the weeds," Maddie told Angus. "You handle the grass."

Maddie walked down one row, pulling up dandelions and other weeds. Angus followed her, nibbling the grass. In minutes, they'd finished the first row.

"Piece of cake!" Maddie said. "Why didn't I think of this before?"

They were about to start down the next one when Dad came running over. "Maddie! Stop! What are you doing?" he cried.

"We're weeding the garden. Angus is helping," she explained.

"But he's trampling the plants!" Dad said.

Uh-oh. Maddie looked back. Behind them lay a row of ruined lettuce. Angus's dinner-plate-size hooves had flattened the tender heads.

"Oops," said Maddie. "Sorry, Dad."

Dad rubbed his forehead. "We'll save what we can. But from now on, Maddie," he added, "please try to keep the horse *out* of the garden."

Angus's ears flopped sadly. He ducked his head and sighed.

"Don't worry, Angus," Maddie said as she led him

29

away. "It was an honest mistake. But you know what you *can* help with—the laundry!"

Near the house, clothes and bedsheets were hanging on a clothesline. It was Maddie's job to take in the dry laundry.

"I'll take them down, and you can carry them," Maddie told Angus.

Maddie unpinned a sheet. She laid it across Angus's back. She added a pillowcase. "This is way better than dragging a laundry basket around," she said.

Soon a heap of laundry was piled on Angus. When the pile was high, Maddie started toward the house, and Angus followed. He didn't notice the clothesline in front of his chest. Angus walked right through the clothesline, snapping it. All the clean laundry landed in the dirt.

"Oh no!" Maddie whispered. "Quick! Help me pick it up—"

"Maddie, what on earth?" Mom said as she came hurrying over. "How did all the laundry end up on the ground?"

"It was an accident," Maddie said.

Mom folded her arms. "Accidents happen. But you're in charge of washing everything again. And do those, too, while you're at it," she said, pointing to the sheets on Angus's back. "No one wants to sleep in a bed that smells like a horse."

"Got it," Maddie said with a sigh. As she led Angus away, she whispered, "I happen to think you smell very nice."

But Angus's big head hung low and his long tail drooped.

Maddie and Angus carried the dirty clothes to

the house so Maddie could start the laundry. On the way back to the barn, they passed Ramsey's pen. Evie was trying to put hay in the ornery goat's trough. But every time she got close, Ramsey butted the fence.

"Cut it out, you grumpy goat!" Evie hollered. "Can't you see I'm trying to feed you?"

Ramsey glared at her and butted the fence again.

"You have to watch out for Ramsey," Maddie explained to Angus. "He tries to head-butt everyone."

But Angus was curious. He wandered closer to Ramsey's pen.

When the goat saw the enormous horse coming

toward him, he gave a single bleat and passed out cold.

The girls stared.

"He's dead!" Evie shrieked. "Angus killed him!"

"He's not dead. At least, I don't think so. He probably

just fainted." Maddie picked up a stick. She poked it through the fence and prodded the goat.

Sure enough, Ramsey's eyes blinked open. He hopped to his feet and trotted straight to the back of his pen.

"There. Now you can feed him," Maddie said to Evie. "Wasn't that helpful of Angus?"

"I guess so." Evie looked at Ramsey. He was staring off into space, pretending not to see the big scary horse. "Poor Ramsey."

By the time they made it into the barn, Angus's head was hanging so low, his big white nose nearly brushed the ground.

Maddie got out a brush and curry comb. Maybe a little grooming would cheer them *both* up.

"Don't worry. Tomorrow will be better," she murmured to Angus as she ran the comb over his thick black fur.

"At least," she added, almost to herself, "I sure hope so."

"The chickens are coming! The chickens are coming!"

Maddie looked up from the stall, where she was saddling Angus. She could see Evie out in the barnyard. She was running in circles and yelling her head off. She looked a little like a chicken herself.

Evie peeked into the barn. "Maddie, did you hear? The chickens are coming!"

"I heard. I think they heard you in Antarctica," Maddie said. "What are you wearing?"

Evie looked down at her clothes. She was wearing a puffy yellow princess gown and an enormous feather boa. Yellow rubber boots stuck out from beneath her skirt.

"It's my *Welcome, chickens* outfit," she explained.

Maddie blinked. "You dressed up . . . for the *chickens?*"

"I want them to feel special. Come on, Maddie. Mom's almost back!" Evie dashed away.

Maddie finished cinching the girth around Angus's middle. "Well, I guess we should go out and see them."

Angus shook his forelock out of his eyes and nickered, as if to say, *Lead the way.*

As they came outside, Mom's pickup truck was just pulling in. Wire crates filled the back.

Mom hopped down from the cab. "Come help unload!" she called.

Maddie tied Angus's lead to the fence. Then she went over to the truck. Dad, Mom, Maddie, and Evie lifted the crates down from the truck bed.

Evie squatted down beside one of the cages. She peeked at the yellow hen inside.

"Do they have names?" she asked.

"I thought you could name them," Mom said.

"I'm going to call this one Cinderella," Evie said.

She pointed at another chicken with white feathers. "And that one should be Snow White."

"Good names," Mom said, smiling.

"Fit for a princess," Dad agreed. "Or a chicken."

By the time the truck was unloaded, Evie had named the other hens Belle, Aurora, Ariel, and Jasmine.

The last chicken had copper-colored feathers and a stubborn look in her eye. "This one is definitely Merida!" Evie declared. She put her hands on her hips and looked around happily at her new feathered friends. "Look! Cinderella laid an egg!"

As Evie opened the cage to reach for the egg, the chicken darted out.

"Oh no!" Evie yelled. "She's getting away!"

Dad leaned down to catch the runaway hen, but she ran between his legs. Mom and Maddie both tried to grab her. But Cinderella dodged them, too. She sprinted across the yard, headed for the wide-open pasture.

But when she reached Angus, she stopped.

Cinderella looked up at the big horse. Angus lowered his head. He sniffed the chicken, as if to say, *Nice to meet you.*

With a flap of her wings, the hen hopped into the air. She landed on Angus's back.

Everybody laughed. "Well," said Dad, "looks like Cinderella found a friend."

Even Mom was smiling. Maddie's heart lifted. Maybe Mom was finally coming around.

Mom took Cinderella down from Angus's back. "Come here, Evie," she said. "Let me show you how to hold a chicken."

Soon Evie was carrying chickens around the yard proudly, chattering to them like they were her best buds.

Maddie smiled. "Come on, Angus," she said. "Let's go for a ride."

As she bridled Angus and lifted the reins over his head, Maddie saw Mom's frown.

"That horse is too big for you to ride," Mom said.

"Aw, Mom. He's gentle as can be," Maddie said.
"We'll just go for a walk around the pasture."

"Just a walk," Mom agreed reluctantly.

Maddie rolled her eyes. "She's such a worrier,"
she muttered to Angus as she clambered up into
the saddle.

Angus nickered in agreement.

High in the saddle, though, Maddie wondered if her mom was right. Angus *was* big. His back was so broad she felt like she was doing splits.

But Angus rode like a dream. He walked a straight line and turned smoothly at the slightest touch of the reins. He didn't pull on the bit or stop to crop grass. He seemed alert to Maddie's every signal.

They did two slow laps around the pasture. It seemed like a shame not to see what more he could do. Surely they could go a little faster?

"Giddyup, Angus," Maddie said, giving him a squeeze with her legs.

As Angus broke into a trot, then a smooth canter, Maddie thought about Princess Merida. How lucky Merida was to have Angus. Maddie pictured them galloping through the wilds of some faraway kingdom and felt a pang of envy. Would Maddie ever have a horse like that?

Out of nowhere, something came flying toward

them. Angus spooked. His head jerked up. He twisted his body sideways, hooves skittering backward. Maddie flew forward in the saddle.

Suddenly she was falling. It felt like a long, *long* way to the ground.

She landed so hard it knocked the wind out of her. The next thing she knew, Mom and Dad were at her side.

"Are you hurt?" Dad asked. "Can you move your arms and legs?"

Maddie tried and found she could. She was bruised. But she could tell she wasn't badly hurt.

When they knew she was okay, her parents helped her stand up. Angus nosed her, as if to say, *Are you all right?*

"I knew this was a bad idea," Mom said. "We aren't ready to have a horse. And this one is just too big for you, Maddie."

"It's okay, Mom. I'm okay," Maddie said. But her voice shook and her knees felt wobbly.

Get back on, Maddie told herself. She'd never fallen off a horse before, but she knew that's what you were supposed to do. When you fell off, you got back on.

Maddie looked at the saddle. It was awfully high up. She remembered how far away the ground had seemed when she was falling.

Shake it off, she told herself. *You can do it. Get back in that saddle.*

But she couldn't. For the first time in her life, Maddie was afraid to get on a horse.

Mom and Dad were watching her. "Why don't you take Angus back to the barn," Dad said gently. "He's had a busy day. He looks like he could use some rest."

Maddie nodded. She took Angus's reins and led him away.

CHAPTER
FIVE

In the barn, Angus nudged her again with his nose. He gave a soft snort as if to say, *Forgive me.*

"It's not your fault, Angus," Maddie said. "I wasn't paying attention."

Maddie knew she'd fallen because she'd allowed herself to get distracted. If she'd kept her mind on riding, this wouldn't have happened.

Evie came to the barn. She had the white chicken in her arms.

"Snow White wants me to tell you she's sorry," Evie said.

"For what?" Maddie asked.

"For scaring Angus. Naughty chicken," Evie said, wagging her finger at the bird. Snow White clucked.

So that's why Angus spooked, Maddie thought. "It's okay," she told Evie.

Except it wasn't okay. Every time she thought about riding Angus, she felt a pit in her stomach.

"Actually, it was really scary," she admitted. "And now I'm afraid to get back on. What if I'm too scared to ever ride again?"

Evie looked at her solemnly. "You have to be brave," she said. "Like Princess Merida. Tell yourself you *have* to ride Angus, 'cause if you don't the whole kingdom will—"

"Evie," Maddie cut her off with a sigh. "I really don't feel like playing Princess right now."

Evie went quiet. She petted Snow White. "I could read to you," she offered after a moment. "When I'm sad, sometimes that makes me feel better."

Maddie didn't feel like reading. But she could tell her sister was only trying to help. "Okay," she agreed.

Evie's face brightened. She set Snow White down then climbed the ladder to the hayloft. When she came back she was holding the book of fairy tales. She opened the book and turned to "The Story of Merida."

Maddie looked at the picture on the first page. A girl with a tangle of red curls stood in front of a gray stone castle. She held a bow in one hand. A quiver of arrows hung from her belt.

49

Maddie had seen the picture before. But she'd never noticed the girl's smile or the bold look in her bright blue eyes. She looked like someone who could be a friend.

Evie sat down next to Angus's stall. "'Once upon a time,'" she began, "'in the kingdom of DunBroch, there lived a princess named Merida. . . .'"

Evie was still learning to read, but she knew the stories in her book by heart. Maddie listened as Evie told Merida's story.

Merida's parents, the king and queen of DunBroch, wanted their daughter to get married, as every princess should. They held a contest to find the right prince. Young men traveled across the kingdom to try to win her hand.

But Merida didn't want to marry. So she entered the contest and won, beating all her suitors. This displeased her parents, especially Queen Elinor. She insisted that Merida should choose a husband.

Maddie felt peaceful sitting on the floor of the barn. She could hear Angus quietly munching hay in his stall and Snow White scratching around the barn floor. She watched dust motes rise in a beam of sunlight. After a while, she realized her legs had stopped shaking.

"'Merida knew the will-o'-the-wisps would lead her to her fate,'" Evie read. "'So she rode her horse, Angus, into the forest to follow them. The wisps led Merida to a witch, who gave her a spell to change her mother. Merida thought the spell would change her mother's mind about the marriage. Instead, it turned the queen into a bear!'"

Evie turned the page and gasped.

"Go on," said Maddie.

"There's no more. Maddie, the ending is gone!" Evie showed her the book. The last pages of the story were blank.

"It happened again!" Evie said. "We changed the

story, just like with Maximus. Merida needs Angus
to find her fate and reach her happily-ever-after!"

Maddie's heart sank. They'd kept Angus too
long, though for Maddie it had only seemed like
a moment. But why had Angus come at all? she
wondered. Why did the wishing well keep granting
her wish only to take it away?

"How will we get him back, Maddie?" Evie asked.
"We're out of wishes."

"We have to try again." Maddie felt a twinge of
guilt. She hadn't told Evie the truth about her wish.
"Run to the house and get another penny. I'll bring
Angus and meet you at the well."

As Evie ran off, Maddie coaxed Angus away from
his meal. "Oh, Angus," she said, stroking his face. "I
wish you could stay."

She leaned her forehead against Angus's nose
and closed her eyes. The horse sighed softly.

As they came out of the barn, Maddie saw a

truck and horse trailer parked in front of the house.
Mom was talking to the driver.

The driver opened his door to get out. As it
swung toward her, Maddie saw the words written on
the side: ANIMAL CONTROL.

The man gestured at Angus. "Is this the horse?"

Maddie gasped. She turned to her mom. "You
called *animal control?*"

"I can explain . . ." Mom began.

"I told you, it wasn't Angus's fault! Why don't
you ever believe me?" Maddie cried.

Without thinking, she put her foot in the stirrup
and swung herself into Angus's saddle.

High on the horse's back, Maddie glanced down at the ground. Her stomach lurched.

Don't look down, she told herself. She was scared of falling. But she was more scared of what might happen to Angus.

Just then, the screen door of the house slammed open. Evie came out, waving a penny. "Maddie, I got it!"

Maddie watched them all come toward her— Mom, Evie, and the man from animal control. Anger bubbled up inside her.

I always do what everyone else wants, she thought. *I try to make everyone happy. But I never get to do what I want. And I want to keep Angus!*

Maddie turned Angus around. She rode past the well and kept on going, headed for the woods. She could hear her mom calling her name. But she didn't stop.

Together, she and Angus raced away.

CHAPTER
SIX

Maddie and Angus galloped through the trees. But Maddie hardly saw where they were going through her tears.

How could she? Maddie fumed. How *could* she?

How could Mom send Angus away just because of one accident? Why did Mom only see the problems with Angus? Why couldn't she see the good things, too?

At some point, Maddie realized that Angus had slowed to a walk. She halted him and looked around.

She was in a part of the woods where she'd never been before. Rays of sunlight shone between the tree branches. The silver-tipped grass rustled.

Maddie hesitated, unsure which way to go. She didn't want to get lost. But if she went back to the farm now, they'd take Angus away.

You have to be brave, like Princess Merida, she heard Evie say.

But what would Merida do?

Out of the corner of her eye, Maddie saw something flicker in the air. She gasped and ducked her head.

It was only a small blue butterfly. It flitted across Maddie's path, then flew off.

Maddie laughed at herself.

"Scared of a butterfly?" she murmured. "So much for being brave."

Two more butterflies darted up from the grass. They chased each other through the air. *Follow us!* they seemed to say.

Angus suddenly gave a surprised snort.

"What is it?" Maddie asked. Then she looked ahead and gasped.

A line of butterflies made a trail through the woods.

It's just a coincidence, Maddie told herself. *It doesn't mean anything. The woods are probably full of butterflies.*

But she couldn't help thinking of the will-o'-the-wisps in Merida's story. Were the butterflies there to lead her to her fate?

Before moving to Horsetail Hollow, Maddie had not believed in magic. That had changed when she threw her first coin into the wishing well. Now magic seemed to be everywhere.

"What do you think, Angus?" she whispered. "Should we follow them?"

Angus shifted his feet. He snorted uncertainly.

"I know what Merida would do," Maddie said. She gave Angus a gentle kick, and they started forward.

Each time they reached a butterfly, it flew off. But another was always just ahead.

The will-o'-the-wisps had led Merida to a witch, Maddie remembered. She didn't think there were witches in the woods around Horsetail Hollow. But her heart beat fast all the same.

As they came through the trees, the last butterfly flew away. Ahead, Maddie saw a house.

The house looked perfectly ordinary. It was small and white. A basket of flowers hung from the porch. Beside it, Maddie saw a fenced pasture with a run-in shelter.

Just a house. Nothing magical about it. Maddie was surprised at how disappointed she felt.

Angus's ears flicked forward. He whinnied loudly.

Another whinny replied. A bay gelding trotted out from behind the shelter, followed by a dapple-gray mare. The two horses came right to the fence to look at Maddie and Angus.

"Well, are you just going to stand there?" a voice said. "Or are you going to say hello?"

Maddie jumped. A woman had come out of the house. She was standing on the porch, watching Maddie curiously.

"H-hello," Maddie stuttered. The woman had a small, round, wrinkled face and dark eyes. Her long gray hair hung in a braid down her back.

"You must be Maddie from Horsetail Hollow," the woman said. "I've been expecting you."

CHAPTER
SEVEN

Maddie sucked in her breath. How did the woman know her name? "Are you a witch?" she blurted.

The woman raised her eyebrows. Then she chuckled. "Not last I checked. I'm Rosalyn, your neighbor."

Maddie's cheeks went hot. Oh boy. She'd called her neighbor a witch!

Rosalyn didn't seem to mind. She stepped off the porch and came toward Maddie and Angus. "That's quite a horse you have," Rosalyn said. "We don't see many draft horses around here. May I say hello?"

Maddie nodded. "His name is Angus," she said.

"Nice to meet you, Angus." Rosalyn held out her hand. Angus touched it gently with his nose, as if to say, *Nice to meet you, too.*

Rosalyn petted him. "He sure is a handsome fellow," she said. "Over there are Stretch and Genie." She pointed to the two horses, who were watching curiously.

"Can I say hello to them?" Maddie asked.

"Go right ahead. They like visitors," Rosalyn said.

Maddie slid down from Angus's back. She walked over to the fence, and held out a hand in greeting. The mare's nostrils flared. She snuffled Maddie's shirt. Maddie giggled.

Rosalyn smiled. "She's looking for a treat. Sometimes I keep one in my shirt pocket."

Maddie petted the mare. "She's so pretty."

"Didn't use to be," Rosalyn told her. "They were skin and bones when they first came to me. Their manes looked like straw. Saddest sight you ever saw."

"Why?" Maddie asked. "What was wrong with them?"

"They hadn't been cared for," Rosalyn explained. "Some folks think they want a horse, but they don't realize how much work it takes. Or they can't afford to feed them. Or maybe their heart just isn't in it. You gotta have a big heart to love a horse."

"Then I guess my mom has a small heart," Maddie said bitterly. "She doesn't like horses."

"Is that so?" Rosalyn raised her eyebrows. "Funny, I got a different impression."

"You know my mom?" Maddie asked.

"We've talked once or twice. I hear you've been having a problem with strange horses. They keep turning up on your farm." Rosalyn's dark eyes studied Maddie.

Maddie suddenly had the feeling that Rosalyn

had guessed where Angus had come from. But how could she?

"Your mom called me for advice," Rosalyn went on. "What kind of food do horses need? What tools? How do you know when to take them to the vet? For someone who doesn't like horses, she asked a lot of questions about how to take care of them."

Mom had done that? It occurred to Maddie that she'd had everything she needed to take care of Maximus and then Angus. Maybe her mom cared more than she ever knew.

"Angus isn't my horse," Maddie admitted. "I got him . . . well, it was sort of an accident. And now he really needs to go home. But I don't want to say good-bye to him yet."

Maddie wasn't sure why she was saying all this. But there was something about Rosalyn that made her feel like talking.

"All my life, I've wanted my own horse," she went on. "A horse that I can feed and groom and ride. But my mom doesn't think I can do it. And now it seems like the universe is sending horses to me, but I can't keep them. It isn't fair!" Maddie felt tears well up in her eyes.

Rosalyn looked at her sympathetically. "There's no better friend in the world than a good horse," she said.

Maddie nodded. Finally someone understood!

"It took a long time for Stretch and Genie to trust me," Rosalyn said. "But now they're each a part of me. I can't imagine how I'd feel if I lost them."

Maddie thought of Princess Merida. Was Angus part of her, too? Maddie guessed so. Without Angus, Merida wouldn't be—*couldn't* be—the brave, adventurous girl she was. She would be just another princess stuck in a castle.

Rosalyn smoothed her hand over Angus's coat and smiled at Maddie. "Come visit me anytime. Genie and Stretch will be happy to see you. And I could always use a hand taking care of them."

"Really?" Maddie asked.

"Of course. Us horse lovers have to stick together," Rosalyn said with a wink.

The thought of coming back boosted Maddie's spirits. "I guess I should take Angus home now," she said.

"There's a path right through those trees," Rosalyn said, pointing. "It's an old horse trail. It will take you where you need to go."

Maddie climbed onto Angus's back. As they turned to leave, she thought of something. "You said you were expecting me. How did you know I was coming?"

"Your mom called. She asked me to keep an eye out for you," Rosalyn told her. She waved, and Maddie waved back. Angus whinnied his good-bye.

Maddie and Angus followed the horse trail. The way back seemed much shorter. In no time at all, they arrived at Horsetail Hollow.

The trail ended at the wishing well. As they approached, Maddie heard someone crying. She got down from Angus.

Evie was sitting next to the well, holding the book of fairy tales. Her princess gown was rumpled. Tears streaked her face.

When she saw Maddie, Evie jumped up and hugged her. "I thought you ran away."

"No," Maddie said, hugging her back. "Well, almost. I'm sorry. I wanted to keep Angus. But now I know what we have to do."

Evie shook her head. "We can't make a wish."

"Sure we can," Maddie said. "I'll bet this time it will work—"

"No, Maddie. *Look*."

Evie pointed to the well. A heavy cement lid covered the opening.

"Where did this come from?" Maddie exclaimed.

"I don't know," Evie said.

"Mom and Dad must have put it on, after we showed them the well," Maddie said. "Come on, Evie. Help me move it."

The girls tried pushing the cover. They tried pulling it. But the cover wouldn't budge.

"It's no use." Maddie slumped against the side of the well. Evie did, too.

"This is all my fault," the girls said in unison.

They looked at each other. "*Your* fault?" Maddie said.

"I wished for Angus," Evie admitted. "He wouldn't be here if it wasn't for me."

Maddie was stunned. "Why?"

"We had so much fun with Maximus," Evie explained. "Going into the storybook and meeting Rapunzel. I wanted to do it all again."

"But then why didn't you just wish us into a fairy tale?" Maddie asked. "Why wish Angus here?"

"Because you wanted a horse. And I wanted to go with you," Evie said. "I'm sorry, Maddie."

"It's my fault, too," Maddie said. "When you tried to wish Angus back to his fairy tale, I didn't make the same wish. I wished for him to stay. And now he can never get home."

Angus lowered his head. He nudged Maddie with his nose, as if to say, *Please don't cry.*

"Oh, Angus," Maddie said. "I'm sorry. If it weren't for us, you'd be in your fairy tale, saving the day—"

Maddie jumped up. "That's it. *We* can't move the cover. But I bet a big strong Shire horse can!"

Maddie ran to the barn and found a rope. She tied one end to Angus's saddle. She tied the other end to the handle on the well cover.

"Pull, Angus!" she cried.

Angus dug his hooves into the ground and pulled. And slowly the cover moved. It was only a few inches. But it was enough.

Quickly Maddie untied the rope. "Do you still have the penny?" she asked Evie.

Evie held up the shiny coin. Then she placed the book of fairy tales on the side of the well, open to Merida's story.

Maddie put her hand on Evie's. She held Angus's reins in her other hand. The sisters closed their eyes and made their wish.

We wish to send Angus back to his story.

As the wind started to blow, Maddie felt hopeful. Maybe, just maybe, they would make it in time.

CHAPTER
EIGHT

Maddie, Evie, and Angus were standing in a moonlit wood. Patches of mist clung to the pine trees. The air was cool and damp. Looking up, Maddie saw hard, bright stars scattered across a blue-black sky. She rubbed the goose bumps on her arms.

"Where's the castle?" Evie asked.

They looked in every direction. But all they saw was forest.

Something nagged at the back of Maddie's mind.

"What else happens in Merida's story?" she asked Evie. "Is there something about a wicked bear?"

"Mor'du. The demon bear," Evie whispered.

"Demon bear?" Maddie felt the hairs rise on the back of her neck.

An owl hooted, making them jump. The girls huddled closer to Angus. His warm, strong body and horsey smell made Maddie feel better. But only a little.

"We should try to find Merida's castle," she said.

But they didn't move. They didn't know which way to go. What if they found Mor'du instead?

Suddenly, Angus gave an alarmed snort and stepped back.

"Look!" Evie gasped.

A ghostly blue light hovered in the air. It seemed to whisper to them.

"It's a will-o'-the-wisp!" Evie reached to touch it, but the light winked out. Looking ahead, Maddie saw the wisps made a wavering trail through the woods.

"They lead you to your fate. We have to follow them!" Evie said.

"Wait." Maddie held her back. "How do we

know if it's a *good* fate or a *bad* fate? What if they lead us to the witch? Or . . . something worse." The thought of Mor'du somewhere in the dark made her heart hammer.

Evie hesitated. Then a determined look crossed her face. "We have to be brave. Like Merida," she said.

Maddie swallowed hard. Brave was the last thing she felt. But she knew Evie was right. Merida was somewhere out there, and she needed Angus.

She took the horse's reins. "Come on then, Angus."

Angus gave a wary snort. But as Maddie and Evie started toward the trail of blue light, he came reluctantly behind.

Following the wisps was like chasing smoke. Each time the girls reached one, it vanished, only to reappear ahead. The wisps wound through the trees and over a rise. There, just ahead, stood Castle DunBroch.

The castle sat at the edge of a cliff, overlooking a dark sea. It was made of cold, gray stones, but warm light shone from the windows.

Relief flooded through Maddie. The wisps had led them to the castle—and to Merida!

Maddie quickened her pace. "Come on! We're almost there!" she cried.

A narrow stone bridge connected the forest to the village and castle grounds. But just as they reached it, Angus gave a shrill whinny of fear.

A hulking shape came out of the darkness. In the moonlight, Maddie could just make out the powerful body and sleek fur of an enormous bear.

Maddie gasped. "It's Mor'du!"

The bear came toward them with astonishing speed. It was almost to the bridge.

Maddie turned to flee. But Evie was right behind her. Maddie ran into her, knocking them both to the ground.

Suddenly Angus stepped in front of them. He was protecting them!

The bear's footsteps shook the ground. It passed

so close to them that Maddie could hear it panting. Then it disappeared into the dark forest.

For a moment, Maddie was too stunned to move. She couldn't believe it. Mor'du had gone right past them. Angus had saved the day!

Slowly, Maddie climbed to her feet. She put her arm around Angus's neck. She could feel him trembling.

Evie was still curled in a tight ball on the ground. Angus nudged her with his nose as if to say, *Are you all right?*

"Evie, it's okay. You can get up now," Maddie told her.

Evie sat up. When she saw the bear was gone, she threw her arms around her sister. "You saved me from Mor'du!"

"It was Angus. He just—" Maddie broke off. She could hear voices shouting. "What's that?"

As they looked at the castle, the gate rose. A horde of men and dogs spilled out. Some of the men carried torches. Others held swords or bows and arrows. The dogs dashed around their feet, barking in a frenzy.

"What are they doing?" Maddie asked.

"Oh no!" Evie's eyes suddenly widened. "They're hunting the bear!"

"That's good, right?" Maddie said. "We want them to catch Mor'du."

"That bear wasn't Mor'du," Evie said. "It came *from* the castle. That bear was Merida's mother, Queen Elinor!"

They watched the crowd stream toward them. In moments, they would reach the bridge.

"We can't let them catch her. Maddie, *do* something!" Evie cried.

What can I do? I'm only a kid, Maddie thought. *How can I stop a mob of angry warriors?*

Then she thought, *We can't stop them. But maybe we can fool them.*

"Come on!" she said, running back toward the woods. "I have an idea!"

In the shelter of the trees, Maddie whispered her idea to Angus and Evie. The horse turned both his ears to Maddie. He seemed to be listening closely. But had he understood?

Angus dipped his head, as if in a nod. *Got it*, he seemed to say.

The sisters watched from behind a tree as Angus galloped away. As the mob came over the bridge, Angus ran right toward them. He whinnied shrilly.

A great, bearlike man with a bristling red

mustache led the mob. When he saw Angus, he held up an arm. "Hold on!"

"It's King Fergus!" Evie whispered to Maddie.

"A horse with nae rider." Fergus spoke with a thick accent. He raised his torch. His eyes widened. "'Tis Merida's horse!"

A surprised murmur ran through the crowd. *The princess's horse!*

Fergus tried to catch Angus's reins. But the horse shied away. Angus's eyes rolled. His nostrils flared. He shivered and shook.

Good job, Angus, Maddie thought. If she hadn't known better, she'd have guessed the horse was terrified.

"He's near scared tae death," Fergus said.

"Nae doubt he crossed paths wit' th' bear," said a barrel-chested man with blond pigtails. "An' barely escaped wit' his life."

"But what's he doing out 'ere at night? And wit' his saddle on," Fergus said. "Merida's the only one that rides him. . . ."

A look of horror crossed Fergus's face as it dawned on him. "Merida's out here somewhere! But how can she be? I locked her safe in the castle myself!"

The crowd seemed to grow uneasy. "There be strange things happening this night," said a stout man with gray hair.

The king waved the crowd forward. "Come on, men! She can't be far off. We must find the bear and save the princess!"

"But the hounds say the bear went thataway," said a skinny man who was holding a hound by its collar. The dog barked and pulled in the direction Elinor-Bear had run.

Fergus glowered down at him. "Who do you believe? Your dog or your king? Merida's horse came from that way. And that's the way we'll go!"

He raised his torch high, calling out, "Merida! Hold tight, lass. We're coming for ya!"

The mob stormed into the woods. Maddie and Evie shrank down behind the tree as they passed.

When the men were gone, the girls ran to Angus. They petted him and praised him. "That was amazing!" Maddie cried. Oh, she was going to miss this horse! But there was no time to think about that now.

"We've got to find Merida," Evie said. "She has to break the curse before it's too late!"

Maddie boosted Evie onto Angus's back. She pulled herself up behind. Together they raced toward the castle.

As they passed through the open gate, Angus whinnied loudly. But this time it was a cry of joy. He was home!

Inside the castle walls, Maddie hesitated. There were so many different buildings. But Angus seemed to know where to go. He trotted toward a low stone building with a wooden fence around it. From inside, there came the sound of frightened whinnies.

At the door of the stable, Angus stopped. Maddie and Evie slid down from his back. By the light of the torches, they took in the scene inside.

A teenage girl with thick red curls was struggling with a gray mare. She was trying to load a heavy tapestry onto the horse's back. But the mare kept spooking.

"Hold still, you useless nag!" the girl cried in frustration. "Can't you see they're just me brothers under a spell?"

Who does she mean? Maddie wondered. Then she saw them. Three little bear cubs stood in the shadows at the girl's feet. The mare was terrified of the cubs. She reared and struggled, her eyes rolling with fear.

"Merida!" Evie cried.

The red-haired girl turned at the sound of her name. When she saw Maddie and Evie, her blue eyes widened.

"Who're you?" she asked. "Where did'ja come from?"

"I'm Evie! And this is my big sister, Maddie." Evie clasped her hands and fixed the princess with an adoring gaze. "Merida, I named a chicken after you!"

"Never mind that," Maddie said. "We're here to help. We brought Angus!"

"Angus?" Merida stared at Maddie. Then she pushed past her, crying, "Angus!"

The horse whinnied joyfully.

"Oh, Angus! Ye beauty!" Merida took his face in her hands and kissed his nose.

Maddie felt a lump in her throat. She could see

now that this was where Angus belonged. He was Merida's horse, and she was his girl.

"He's a really good horse," she told Merida.

"Aye, he is," Merida agreed.

"If I ever have a horse, I want him to be just like Angus. Though my *mother* will probably never let me," she added bitterly.

"Don't speak ill of yer mum," Merida said in a quiet voice.

Maddie shook her head. "She doesn't understand me."

"Then ye must give her the chance to. Or someday ye might find it's too late." Tears welled in Merida's eyes. She wiped them away impatiently. "I've got to go."

The princess swung onto Angus's back, pulling the tapestry with her. The three little bears scrambled up the tapestry to sit with Merida. Then they all galloped away into the night.

Maddie and Evie watched them go. "Do you think they'll make it?" Evie asked.

"I hope so," Maddie said. Her chest felt tight.

Evie looked at her. "Are you sad about Angus?"

"A little." Maddie swiped at her eyes. "I was actually thinking about Mom."

Evie took her hand. "Let's go home, Maddie."

"Oh no." Maddie suddenly had a sinking feeling. "How are we going to get there?"

"I have another penny!" Evie said.

"What good is a penny without the wishing well?" Maddie said.

Her eyes fell on the gray mare. She was saddled and ready to ride. *Maybe we can borrow her,* Maddie thought. *Just to find the well, and then . . .*

"Don't even think about it," Evie said. "From now on, let's leave fairy-tale horses in their stories. Okay?"

"Okay," Maddie agreed. They would have to figure out some other way back to Horsetail Hollow.

As they walked out of the stables, Maddie suddenly stopped. "Look at that," she said.

The wishing well was standing in the middle of the courtyard. It looked like it had been there hundreds of years.

"What's it doing here?" Evie asked.

Maddie smiled. "I think it's here to take us home."

CHAPTER

TEN

Moments later, the girls were back in Horsetail Hollow. The sun shone brightly, as if no time had passed. They were standing beside the wishing well. Someone else was there, too.

"Mom?" Maddie said.

Mom had her back to them, but she spun around when she heard Maddie's voice. Her face flooded with relief.

"Oh, girls! I didn't hear you walk up," she said.

Maddie went to her mom and put her arms around her. Mom looked surprised. Then she hugged Maddie back.

"I was so worried," she murmured into Maddie's hair.

"I know," Maddie said. "I'm sorry."

"Me too," said Mom.

"Me three!" Evie wrapped her arms around both of them. "Hug sandwich!"

They stayed that way for a long moment. Then Mom looked around. "Where's Angus?" she asked.

"He had to go home," Maddie said.

"Home?" Mom looked confused. She glanced at the book lying open on the side of the well. Then her eyes widened in wonder. "What in the world . . . ?"

In the picture, Princess Merida stood in front of Castle DunBroch. She looked out from the page with laughing blue eyes. She still held a bow in one hand. But now her other hand rested on a horse—a handsome black Shire with a white blaze on his forehead.

"I'm sorry I ran away," Maddie said.

Mom tore her eyes away from the book. "Oh, Maddie. I'm the one who's sorry. I shouldn't have called animal control without telling you."

"Angus wasn't dangerous," Maddie said. "It's not his fault I fell."

"I know," Mom said. "It wasn't the fall, sweetheart. At least, it wasn't *only* that. It was . . . Well, you've wanted a horse so badly. I could see how much you adored Angus. But he wasn't ours to keep. I was afraid the longer he stayed, the more crushed you'd be when he had to go." She sighed. "I just wanted to protect you. But I went about it all wrong."

I got it wrong, too, Maddie thought. All along she'd thought her mom hated Angus. But really she was just worried about Maddie.

"But what are you doing here at the . . . well?" Maddie caught herself before she said *the wishing well.*

A funny look crossed Mom's face. "I made a wish," she admitted.

The sisters looked at her in amazement. "You *do* believe the wishing well is magic!" Evie exclaimed.

Mom smiled. "Maybe I do. After all, my wish came true."

"What did you wish for?" Maddie asked.

"I wished for you home safe and sound." Mom put one arm around Maddie and the other around Evie. "Come on, let's go tell Dad you're back."

As they walked toward the farmhouse, Maddie glanced back at the well. Maybe sometime they'd have another adventure. But for now she was glad to be home.